DIGITAL DIGIMON MONSTERS ™

☀ TAI

THE OFFICIAL SCRAPBOOK

Ladybird

Hello, I'm Tai!

Koromon

Agumon

Greymon

...and these are my new Digimon friends! Wait until you hear how I met them!

ONE DAY AT SUMMER CAMP, A WEIRD THING HAPPENED...

It started to snow – and we
were somehow transported to...

DIGIWORLD!!!

I didn't know where I was – or what this thing was in my hand!

I later found out it was a Digivice.

The first thing I saw when I looked around was this little fellow. Luckily, he was friendly. His name is Koromon, which means 'Brave Little Warrior'.

Here in DigiWorld, Koromon tries hard to help me! He's my own personal Digimon! Sometimes we have to make a run for it!

MY HUMAN FRIENDS:

Some of the other kids who went to camp with me ended up in DigiWorld, too!

Matt

He's a good kid, but can be very stubborn.

T.K.

Matt's little brother. T.K. works hard to keep up with us.

8

Izzy

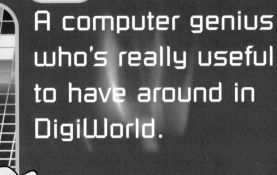

A computer genius who's really useful to have around in DigiWorld.

Sora

She's like a sister to me – and looks out for everybody!

Joe

Smart, but worries about everything!

Mimi

She's really great – even if she would rather go shopping!

GOOD DIGIMON:

We found out that Digimon can be good – or bad. Here are some of the good ones that have become our own personal protectors!

Motimon
Izzy's Digimon

Tsunomon
Matt's Digimon

Yokomon
Sora's Digimon

Koromon
My Digimon

Tokomon

T.K.'s Digimon

Bukamon

Joe's Digimon

Tanemon

Mimi's Digimon

We all seem to have a knack for trouble...

KOROMON DIGIVOLVES!!!

D'you know what's really cool about Digimon? They Digivolve!

Through the mystical powers of our Digivices, whenever we need help or protection, the Digimon Digivolve into strong warriors in the battle against evil! The first stage they Digivolve to is called 'Rookie'.

We couldn't believe our eyes when
we saw our Digimon Digivolving to
Rookies to fight Kuwagamon, the
giant beetle-like monster!

Meet my amazing Rookie
Digimon, Agumon! He
Digivolved from Koromon.

AGUMON HAS A SECRET WEAPON

"Pepper Breath!"

That fiery breath of my little friend gets 'em every time. Ouch!

He can even start campfires...

And thaw out frozen clothes!

MY DIGIVICE AND HOW TO USE IT

When I'm in trouble and Agumon needs to Digivolve, my Digivice gets going!

It turns good Digimon into bigger, more powerful fighters, just when I need help most!

The Digivice is an ancient, mystical weapon against evil.

Look how it helped save me from Leomon in a bad mood!

WHEN GOOD DIGIMON TURN BAD

Those Black Gears turn
good Digimon bad...
and when that
happens, look out!

FEAR THE
BLACK
GEAR

Leomon

Once his Black Gear was out,
Leomon told us we were
'Digidestined' to save the world!

Monzaemon

This big teddy bear Digimon
runs a happy Toy Town – until
he gets a Black Gear in him!

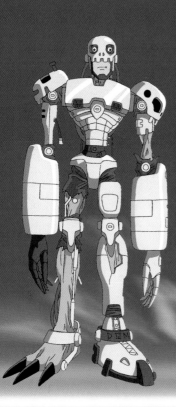

Andromon

Andromon helped us escape from an old factory after we got the Black Gear out of his leg.

Meramon

A good Digimon who guards a volcano. He attacked us until we got his Black Gear out.

Frigimon

This giant snowman attacked me and Agumon in Freeze Land. After we got his Black Gear out, he helped us find Matt.

When we get the Black Gears out, the bad Digimon become good again.

Joe had quite a ride getting the gear out of Unimon!

Unimon

MY CREST: COURAGE

Gennai told us we each had a crest. When we found our crests, our Digimon could Digivolve to even higher levels.

Gennai

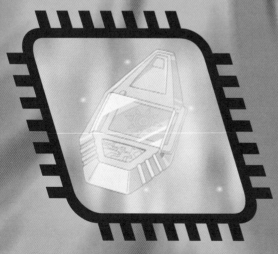

There are lots of different lands in DigiWorld, like File Island, Primary Village and Infinity Mountain. I found my crest in a cave on the continent of Server!

BIGGEST AND BEST BATTLES EVER!

Kuwagamon had teeth like knives – and scissor hands!

I thought this Digimon had me for certain!

I thought we'd never get out of Etemon's Pyramid!

Greymon turned Shellmon into fish bait!

Greymon vs. Leomon!

Frigimon gets ugly!

Devimon blew us away, but we soon got back on track!

Monzaemon has a way of keeping you captive!

Everyone attacked Devimon at once!

Metal Greymon
Giga-BLASTS
Shogunmon!

Datamon sent all these little
bad Digimon after us!

Even an avalanche
can't stop Greymon.

We're sucked
into the vortex!

WHAT'S COOL ABOUT DIGIWORLD

You get to camp with friends.

We learn from the good Digimon (minus their Black Gears)!

It's great when we find something to eat, even just a few trays of eggs!

A swim once in a while is brilliant!

Here's Piximon – isn't he, well... very pixie-ish?

WHAT BUGS ME ABOUT DIGIWORLD

There's NEVER enough to eat!

It's not real, it's digital! (Or is it???)

I really can't stand Gekomon or Numemon...

... they're two disgustingly dirty Digimon!

Do you call this food?

Demidevimon is a real pain!

JUST PLAIN BAD DIGIMON!

Devimon, ruler of the bad Digimon!

These Digimon NEVER have a good side! They are just out to take over DigiWorld – AND the real world... AND they don't care what they have to do to get their way!

Myotismon

Ogremon

Etemon

Devimon

MY BEST HUMAN FRIENDS

Sora is, well... really okay. She might be a kid, but she's pretty grown up, too. She gives me good advice (even if I don't always listen).

I like Matt, but...

Matt and I don't
always agree
on everything.

I think he's more
sensitive than he
lets on, but he
really does act like
a tough guy. Matt
drives me crazy
sometimes!

ALL ABOUT AGUMON

My brave friend
vs. Kuwagamon.

Agumon is always by
my side... and the other
Digimon love him, too.

Uh-oh... is that Ogremon in the next cubicle?

Wearing disguises, Agumon and Palmon quietly sneak into Myotismon's castle!

Piximon shows us how to Digivolve correctly!

To Digivolve, our Digimon have to be very well fed. As we learned from Piximon, they especially need to eat a lot to Digivolve past the Rookie level – to the Champions they are capable of being!

Here's Agumon stuffing in another preparation for the next big Digivolve!

THE GREAT GREYMON!

When I'm in really big trouble and need extra powers, Agumon Digivolves to the Champion level GREYMON.

One of the first Digimon Greymon had to fight was a bad version of himself that Etemon sent to attack us!

As Gennai had told us, in times of great danger our Digimon can evolve even further to their ultimate levels... but they need the

help of our crests to do this. Here my crest does its work and so does Greymon. He Digivolves into Metal Greymon!

NOVA BLAST!!!
Greymon's special weapon is a fire-blast
more powerful than... well, ANYTHING!

NOVA BLAST

Andromon is
no match for
Greymon and
Garurumon!

After we got back to my real world through a digital dimensional warp, Greymon and I had to fight the bad Digimon that Myotismon sent to destroy the Earth!

CAN WE EVER GET BACK TO EARTH?

Sora misses the smell of clean shirts.

Even though we get pulled back at times to fight, it really would be nice to go back home for good.

I want to eat and take a bath!

I wonder how – and what my parents are doing.

I miss my sister, Kari.

I wish I could play football again.

45

THE ADVENTURE CONTINUES...

I know one thing for sure... there's a lot of excitement ahead for all of us!